KATALIYA NAGAR

SUMEET KUMAR

Sumeet Kumar

Sumeet Kumar , A adult who experiences many phases of life , a well known writer and a writer of new era . In reality he is a writter as well as singer (as a hobby) and a standup comedian . Very exciting and interesting fact about him is that he is author of New era i.e. he starts his journey of writing at the age when he was going to schools to get the study . His streak of 100 books will be the great achievement for him in future. His some famous works i.e. Maturity Of Love (Genre - Love),Privacy For Dream (Genre

- Middle Class), Army Squad ofLove (Genre- The Seperation of Army Love), 5 Days of Love(Genre- Temporarily Love), Th e Endearment Of Love(Genre - Historical Era Of Love), Social Destruction Indo-Pak (Genre - The Story of The Love At The Time Of Division Of India And Pakistan), Middle Class Soul (Genre - The Dreams of Middle Class), The Accursed Kanatpur (Genre -The Horrific Story Of A Village), Wrong Number (Genre -The Suspenseful Physco Killer Story), The Secrecy OfDeadly Midnight (Genre - The Suspense About a Crime),Fragile Religious Of Death (Genre- The Death Of A TrustfulPerson), Nature Vs Science (Genre - The Future Battle Between Nature And Science In A Horrific Way), Generic Man (Genre - The Dream of I.I.T), The Unconsious 12 Hours(Genre - The Illusion At Stage Of Comma), The StrangeBurden (Genre - The Burden Of Love) , Her Existence (Genre- The Female Pain In The Society) , Jockstrap Prize (Genre -The True Story Of A National Athlete) , H Man [Hindi] (Genre - Superhero Tragic Story), H Man [English] (Genre - Superhero Tragic Story) , Maturity Of Love [Englsih] (Genre - Love) and many more are available on various geners on the offcial platform of **Amazon, Flipkart and Notionpress.** You can buy them from there.

Contents

ACKNOWLEDGEMENTS

Aman Kumar

Special Thanks to **Aman Kumar** who worked so hard in the preparation of this book. He has continually put with my passive voice, omission of words, and late night calls. You have been wonderful. Thanks to him for his precious time in reviewing proposals , individual chapters and early drafts, along with his suggestions on the applicability of the material to the world.

I

Not to Fortify

There are also some nights that we cannot see in the morning When we try to make two batiob, we don't even know what we have done, because of which our tomorrow's beginning has also turned out to be like our today's and if today's beginning is bad then what is tomorrow's problem? It will be like this too, my daughters may not understand everyone's feet, there are some secrets too, in the world, whose pain remains only as a secret, how much time do we sleep in a day, how many times we say and how much time someone Remember, we don't know this thing at all, whatever we do, we do it with understanding and in the process of thinking and understanding, we are not able to do any work in good health, has anyone ever thought that why it happens like this?

Which is the right habit that compels us to think about our future and who has created the future, is there any such thing? Let us assume that the past is there, is there any such thing, if you want to move forward in your life, then why worry about your future and even care about the past, how does life ever progress, it is not at all such a thing that we move forward We cannot grow, even if we do not say, then our luck will continue to lead us in any way and say this is the right time, this is the wrong time bash cares only about it Why is he never forgotten undefined And if by mistake we get our feet to grow up, then we try to forget him and vow not to remember him and maybe in everyone's gathering, the pain of bad time reflect present time and it tells us that why we ourselves are different from others, the value of time can be known only by the witness who knows that what he lost in his part, who has got the reason for pain instead of right prayer, why he He struggles with his own existence all the time, tries to stay away from himself, tries to fight himself every day, makes many rebellions and asks questions. The anger becomes so much that by saying that the earth can never forget him, is it true that we always increase our spirits beyond the expectation of the world and try to destroy ourselves by doing some things There is also such a thing that I am going to share and it may be right in some way or the other. They live with us all the time, do not eat anywhere and ask us many questions, has anyone ever thought that in reality our life is undefined, what do we say about ourselves and others, who is the story of our true existence by coming to our part.

Hans: He asks what is life? Who should take the right path and move forward in our life, what should we feel about ourselves and others, why do we feel this love for someone else, this is the life of a human being in those questions. There is a fall where he cannot separate himself from them even by saying because the waste of the past will never let him live. Today's world is only a bailout while giving, that too for the sorrow of happiness and also for the waste that if there is a request to return to a journey, then there is no need to choose our destination, we should have the right bash path and if the path is right hot then care about the destination. Who does it, the way the world has been destroyed, it has been destroyed by all the ears, it is nothing but a dream nowadays, well dreams have become such a charity these days, whose education is neither simple nor different. It's better because it's the only thing that if we try to work hard in our life then it will come in our part or else we will lose our happiness time, it is not necessary that what we think about us also Think as much because he sat down for everyone to think. Things are happy, the way is the only one, try to live this thing, people want to die. They choose what they think in advance because when people lose their lives in some sport, they try to kill themselves because that thing gives them comfort and it also takes a lot of power. Thought that why they do not try to live instead of dying, because the day the witness thought that now he cannot fulfill his dreams even after saying that, then he had lost both his life and luck at that happy time. Who is the right life, which he will maintain and who is the right happiness which will be his part again.

I can only do it when people leave their town and come somewhere else, then they come in some other town, so the hope they have at the time, move ahead that too in the beginning it is just like the moon, which we can see. begining for something can never choose the feet because not only do we have the respect to meet them and even if we do, how can we do it, its height is so much that we can't do it.He can't stop his fate from his floor, so he tries to stay away from him. Whenever something good happens to us in this world, it is bad for us above all that it is god for us to maintain our activities and so on.

many times we don't even give them a gift in its affair; Now this gift, which people believe in faith, according to their own faith, they should have the wop of their feet, has anyone ever asked them these things! Lord, we have come to your Saran, if you want something from your devotees, then you must tell the truth, then I do not find this words to be true at all, that even if it happens, it means that no matter how strange it seems that we are asking from a stone. You don't need anything, faith is in the heart, there is only their idol in the stones and today's human beings are also strange and their world is also strange.

Give us some feet, their faith is never complete Take everything, that upper one is not responsible at all, people say that our fate and the vision of the upper person is enough for death, why the day they got angry, we will leave the world and leave the world, which is probably different and probably different. I don't even understand, what I am going to say now, maybe every gift of it will be true, because if the training of thinking is seen, then it will be

Only half of the world has been created by God, the rest of it has been done by his captives, do not understand? The half of the world that we have created, if someone dies in a car accident, then we consider the person responsible for that too and also believe that if the life is saved by the good time, then we will be thankful to them and if by mistake Only the luck was not special and the male witness died at the time, so for that we blame only the above man, so whose fault is it in the human world, which we believe that the male above has created this world which we have The fault is theirs, said they have neither made anything nor do we have any China? So this tomb, which every curve is decided every day, in the end, who has written it, can anyone erase the curse of the question? Still some people may not understand my words, it may be they are thinking of me as crazy and some people have thought this too. Or will it be that what it says in the end, separate it from understanding because its thinking is different, its every person is a jute, atheist: it is undefined maybe my words may be wrong, I am strict somewhere in the wrong undefined foot my words They can never be wrong if the creation of the world is done by the Supreme Lord, then we have tried to make it better by making the world better, and somewhere behind its destruction, we are also involved if we can see it with our own eyes. See, everything that we have made is a waste, we have built houses by cutting pairs, is it right undefined We have also stopped the flow of rivers, is it right undefined We have also given birth to a society which we do not need. Pat Gora art, understanding the color difference, showing love, love, shoes, relationships and many such surgery things, in which even if I write today, I will not be able to write , if a witness dies of a heart attack, then is it the fault of his heart behind this? We will blame the above man for this, he only created the human race, he never gave birth to humanity. Every single family fights today about something that they themselves have made, no one else has created it, has they not given birth to such a thing as hatred, this daluat after which we run on food everyday and because of it As long as they are ready to take someone's life, then the above person has made faith is right, the foot blind faith is absolutely wrong, I am not even saying that the upper one is not present with us in the world, he is present, where is the foot? undefined The mountain which Mahadev considers as his home, has ever been the footprint of a human foot, has any human mountain foot found a stick till date undefined If some donation is true, then it is very far from us, because the age in which it is When Vasudev Krishna, whom we love with great love, is Kanhiya Bullet, who had saved the shame of Draupadi and saved her from being naked, so today, in every street, the respect of our sisters and the respect of daughters is becoming a common sapphire. Then why no one does his bloody undefined where he is as bad as Vasudev, Krishna and left . How was the creation of the world, no one knows, neither does it human race, nor is there any such environment stable in their science which can tell who actually created the world, if I believe everything, then it will be If there is wealth, compulsions and relationships are broken and this cruelty ends soon. Trying to understand us as in the third law of Navaton these words are written clean, undefined every action is opposite reaction. Science also proves to be true when their magnitudes are the same, don't understand the meaning undefined if you don't understand then maybe you understand now Only its shadow is found in the intestine, if you have done virtue with this, then only the feeling of virtue will be transcended in return, and if someone has the courage to ask for trouble, then in return, we will be blessed with the story of trouble. I can forgive many times, foot karma is a very unselfish thing because neither of these things are really related to their relatives and they are no other fear and path.

Their virtues and sins never change, their thinking never changes, who said that our anger and our fear are one, if there is such a thing, then when a common foot is burnt, then why does his anger become free at the same time, why not with him Jalti undefined If two bodies are one life, then how does their anger get separated at the time of death? Knowledge has thought about it, it has been verified by some kind of evidence, what people nowadays consider to be experiments and experiments of science, it is also becomes a prediction.

"JUST CHANGE THE PREDICATION OF LIFE BECAUSE WHEN YOU FORGET TO ALIVE ITS BECOME YOUR LAST RIDE."

If any question has been related in the world, then the beginning of the answer has already been started somewhere or the other, in the request of enough time, his passion is still incomplete, so the story of his existence is still incomplete, well, the secret of his life I'm going to make you all aware that maybe he only hates his passion because his love was murdered the day the darkness started undefined

"I don't need , neither the way nor the wish of the heaven

I neither have tears in my eyes nor looking for the heaven."

Before every handwriting of the word, there are some words which I am going to say to all of you, maybe it can be right and it can also be wrong, its wish may be fulfilled. There is also the right to break the relationship and get better, if you do not show the moments of trouble in someone's world, then that too will be very difficult for your world. Do not feel sorry for killing him because his heart and his life took care of the world, and if someone tried to spoil him at the time, then he might not be able to rock his own humiliation at the same time by saying that to destroy someone. In simple words, we only need to care about our own world and not anyone else's because humanity comes out with time.

II

Mend With Jinx

If someone's dream is incomplete in the world, then someone's love is incomplete, and if we try to progress the journey even further, then this world is incomplete, without fear, there is no existence of happiness, like happiness if it is on the other side. If you see, the reality is only one foot, their saying is different, we try to find the training to move forward every day. Why do they run, now there are many problems of the past that if someone's bad feet are good, then every one of their blessings is really true, if the life of a person is a prayer, then it is inevitable that the baddua is also theirs. Every one is included in unconscious world , if there is good and then there is also evil, if one has started walking like a traveler, then many such nights come in it, which can take you to your destination and go somewhere far away from it. Still, we never stop walking on them, hope is such that it only makes a person hollow inside, even if every sixth of his outside is in your existence. Trying to move forward, his bail does not work because of his death, because nowadays everyone has felt that he is Ranjha, why not only a great lover like Romeo and Juliet. Neither that person can never complete his sleep, nor can he ever try to sleep, this debate does not get lost in itself, have you ever met such a witness, if not, then you all have an IOC floor.

I am going to take the person whose life is also desolate and his anger too. If yes, they used to get ready to destroy every one of their wealth to make him worse, similar was the story of Katliya Nagar, which is probably completely ruined now, if you want to give something to someone in the part, then you Did someone donate clothes, bread, and jewelery to such a witness, whose cruelty made every wall of the city of Katliya sad instead of happy. Kept imprisoned in the dark shadow and gave such an enmity to all of them that their entire world was destroyed in a jiffy if someone's love is not pure and when he loses his life in those enemies of the society. Who will be wrong at the time of the society, this is their love undefined person, why do we forget that against whom we have made him today, somewhere in the past, then why are we trying to erase the happiness bail, if someone's life is lost. If love is wrong, it is also possible, their hatred is also unmatched I am the sixth to ask such questions, that too the human society, which burnt their fear in front of a packed gathering, they could never separate their anger, who has made this rule that if we are a man, only a woman can love. In his place, if a man becomes infatuated with love, then he is wrong in the eyes of the society, his love is wrong, it is a great sin that he has committed.

What is the sin and if a boy wants to love a girl from a different caste, then it doesn't explain us right. Jainism, Buddhism, who is all this? Or is their caste different from us, is their religion different from us, it is written in our Bhagvad Gita, in which book to do this, this prayer has been included in some charity that according to religions And only after seeing the caste system, should we be in love with someone? It is nothing else, when an animal kills another animal, then in its affection we call it as an animal and if a human has killed another human in the same place, then why do we call it human? If someone has been killed by any human race in the universe, then why are we still called human beings? Do not call like this The one whom people also knew by the name of complete desire , he was such a happiness. Once upon a time, even the villagers of the outside used to envy seeing him that why there is such a tradition in our villages, why the logs of our villages cannot remain so happy, there is also a story behind it. What is probably going to come out now is your Sholay movie , in which we had Jai and Veeru, just like this, there are two witnesses behind this too, whose love for them was very similar to their feet, their names are Pechan, Arsh and Akhilya Seh. Both used to refer to different religions, there was such a deep friendship between them that no one in the villages used to call them friends, everyone used to understand that both of them are brothers by birth, let's see some memories of their friendship first. Let's do the Arsh which refers to the Muslim family, and they are related to a Hindi religion, this food may be 1925.

It is said that when the film Sholay had not even come, it was a matter of time before our country had got freedom, Kataliya Nagar was such a city where people were always ready to help each other. King Ram Lakhan Pratap of Hasrat Purr also loved the person of complete desires because the
the complete desire , I am talking about was made in his memories only after the death of his Begum, whom he loved very much. There were no high jobs, when Raja Ram Lakhan Pratap called him, he would go to tour and appear in front of him, Arsh and Akhilya had also taken birth, the feet of their parents were just as soon as they gave birth. It was because at that time the neighboring kingdom was attacked in the city of Katliya, in which Arsh and Akhilya's father was also involved in the memory, meaning he was with his king Ram Lakhan Pratap at the time when the news of his death was heard by Arsh and Akhilya's mother.

When told to, she could not poison the accident and finally she gave her life. They were very close and their friendship was also so deep that when he died, his fear was buried together instead of being burnt, that too the same grave where even today person listen to the stories of their friendship, Akhila's father was a Hindu. Why was buried instead of the question which is now in your part, it was started long ago by some people, Akhila's father always used to say that if I die, then I should be buried where I have spent all those memories of my childhood. I have made it with my only friend, after the burning of my head, it is possible that my soul should also leave the magnificence of the spark with me somewhere, so I say that even my courage should be blessed with a happy grave where I kill myself.

I could also stay close to my friend, feet maybe their paths were different, feet were the same, their destination was the same because the death of Akhilya's father was a puzzle in the battle, when Arsh's father saw the partive fear of his love friend, he also got angry. She had said goodbye to him at the time, Arsh's father used to say that if either of us had died earlier, then Lord God, my only recommendation is that my death should also be successful at the time of Sajdah. If you will try to say this Pagtal Paan too, then some logs will also call it a sacrifice. Erased the streak and even his principle, how can we name his valor and relationship only as friendship. Just like his father was very good friend in the past, similarly in the past Arsh and Akhilya also had a deep love for him.

Friendship was neither Akhilya could ever live without Arsh nor Arsh ever without Akhilya, the friendship of both of them was so deep that if one feels younger, then the other also wants to adopt a younger one to feel the pain. Trying to bash in every abuse of the songs, from childhood to youth, both of them grew up playing together and even if they were two There was no mother's affection and father's shadow over them, nor was their love involved, yet both of them were very happy in their life because they were enough for each other and there was no such thing that they did not try to break them. Their friendship was done many times, their friendship was so deep that they never got toad anyone's hatred, even the person of the songs were loved by both of them very much, no matter what happens in the morning, Raja Ram Pratap used to remember him earlier. And Raja Ram Pratap used to say that these two should never be separated because the way his father was a friend and the kind of multiplicity he had shown in the war against the neighboring kingdom and also got him victory, similarly Raja Ram Pratap also used to say . That Arsh and Akhilya should also protect the city of Katliya and became a great soldier like their father, about this, when Raja Ram Pratap called him to his door, at that time Akhilya met Princess Kaveri, who was Kaveri, who was Raja Ram Pratap.

He was also the only fulfillment and his pride and life too, he never used to say that his only daughter should ever have any trouble. That's why he has set a hundred soldiers of his kingdom for their service and has given a strict order that none of them did not talk to the princess. For the first time, Akhliya met Princess Kaveri, the very first time Arsh was also the same foot, the feet whose love was already tire in their fate, their lines cannot be erased even by saying sohush vaat, on one side those harsh principles of King Ram Lakhan There were those who would never adopt their love, they were very ignorant of the don's thing at the time of the first meeting, if someone falls in love with him in the first meeting, he never forgets him till the death of the dam and at the time of the princess's heart and There was a similar stir in Akhilya's heart, even though they had met for a while, the feet might have been a gift of old age, foot Arsh had no idea of the danger that Akhilya was in such a trap. The floor is gone where his mort is sure.Do not stay away when King Ram Lakhan Pratap asked them in front of Arsh and Akhila that do you accept this order that both of you should become a soldier like your father and protect your kingdom, then at the same time both of them have the same words. And he was also about to give birth to a new destruction, when Arsh was asked these things, then at that time Arsh did the same things in front of Raja Ram Lakhan Pratap, which he probably should have also said, because the way both of those fathers had sacrificed their lives for their kingdom. It was given that he did not say that the past should be repeated again, nor did he say to enslave anyone because his world was different and when Akhilya was asked about this, he also said that whatever my friend He has said in front of you that my wish is also the same, all he was going to say that the king asked the rest of the soldiers to make them captive, because at that time both of them had said that too in front of Raja Ram Lakhan Pratap. There were many logs in each of those times, who felt that Arsh and Akhila had worshiped them by disobeying their words , on the orders of their king. has been rejected, it is said that one whose intellect is strong, he may not have the strength, yet he can still win in any battle, the feet whose intellect is only suppressed and he uses only batis, then his harm is better than before it becomes certain.

"I don't care about the time
I don't enlighten my wish
I have found many places in his love for a while.
I should be found left dead was her last wish"

III

Endearment Set Off Recantation

If some things are not in front of anyone, then it is okay that everyone in the world says and says to change the style of their lives, say they are common people, these people who have immense power of power above them, they also say to change their affection. And because they say to change because they feel that they are not better now and the people below them also think that there is a small difference between the castes in the legs, it can also be called a difference, which is the first. Some people say that hard work has been achieved, so some people take the risk of this fraud by shedding blood, just like King Ram Pratap's thinking was similar, he knew the qualities of both of them very well and understood that even though they were the same. They were not great soldiers in the eyes of the villagers because they have never shown their valor and a great warrior is the one who proves his qualities only when he needs it Arsh and Akhil were brave and intelligent like their father. Never used to say that he was tying in some bondage because when his father died and as childhood they both had seen, perhaps they were Deo was refusing them to cross the threshold all the time, maybe there are some things which are still incomplete in the part, it is a mystery that we all will meet soon, the day Arsh and Akhilya have made King Ram Lakhna.

When Pratap's order was rejected, all the logs who were sitting in the meeting ordered that both of them should be taken captive and should also be locked in our yesterday's cell, their king had not given this order at all. Before that, even before he could say anything, the soldiers of kataliya nagar attacked both of them, in the foot, he had said that even though he could not see his powers in front of anyone else, for the first time he used his powers which he had since childhood. He had learned and demonstrated his bravery to all the soldiers present, after all, the respect of the king increased for him even more. That too for Akhilya, who could have become a destruction, later when this incident happened, after that the king gave this order to his soldiers. Said that everyone should go back and after all, Raja Ram Pratap put both of them on his feet It will be known that King Pratap had touched both of them at the same time, then there was a leg behind him, who was the true rivalry of King Ram Lakhan Pratap. If you need anything, then you can come to our court anytime and ask for it and you can do whatever you say in the kingdom, whoever you say, you can kill the limit of his life. Bailout then right foot, the second donation that he received was also a part of his bravery, maybe it was something strange, why did he ruin someone's life and someone's house, why debt means he got cash custody Some fanna is related to her. After all, both of them have gone to then. She was feeling at the time that this is some kind of enmity which can give trouble to us, so at this time she had already said this thing to Akhilya that whatever my friend Raja told us to completely matt my feet trust, maybe it is his There is such a thing that can kill our happiness, even after hearing all this, Akhilya was still lost in the thoughts of Princess Kaveri, because whatever rare thing he had tried to see in the four walls of the room, that memory was in his mind. It was not going to go away so soon and these things then completely turned into reality. For the first time, she met the princess Kaveri, the first day Arsh was not together, nor did she know that Akhilya had fallen in such a trap. The one who is taking her closer to death, everything was fine till the first meeting and even after this, Princess Kaveri and Akhilya met each other many times, they were very unaware of the danger that Raja Ram Lakhan Pratap had come to know about it. And even though the feet were the same, their thoughts were very different. Akhilya loves her and perhaps even further, he would have been very difficult from her if Raja Ram Pratap's minister had not told him these conversation, then why did Akhilya hide these conversation from him, he could have told him if he would have told him because it It happened for the first time that Akhilya had hidden something, and he was also surprised by the fact that if Akhilya has hidden these things from me that he loves princess Kaveri, then there can be some enmity behind this too. undefined Since childhood, they grew up together with each other, played together, faced trouble each other. When the minister of Katliya city said these things to Arsh, at that time he had said one more thing which probably Arsh already knew that after all he did not say at all that Akhilya should now stay in Katliya city, so he told this thing to Akhliya.

Somewhere that we would have to leave the city of Katliya and go, at that time Akhliya did not know at all that the king had to leave his wife.

Dude friend and is trying to hide that too by someone else's saying, he already knows these things, when Arsh told him that now we can not live in Katalia city, then at that time Akhilya questioned him many times. At the time Arsh said to Akhilya that there are some logs of Abu's life in the adjacent town and there is an eye in his house, that's why both of them have called us, at this time Akhliya got an idea that Arsh was someone from him. Trying to hide secret In the part, it was probably going to be full now, as they both were about to leave for the other Sehar, the soldiers of Katliya Nagar were present on their square feet and at the same time Arsh and Akhilya were also aware of the teachings that they were on their square feet. Why the feet have come, Arsh these people knew that they had come to take Akhila only, that's why he said to Akhliya that friend, you should go to the back door and I will be in front, feet are there. Liya refused to obey his instruction for a long time, after that for a long time, Arsh did not even consider the feet of Kosh Singh to understand him, then in the end, I know that the princess and you are very close to each other. Love you and worry, the princess Kaveri is waiting for you at the border of Sahidya Nagar, I will come after you till I see them and she again ordered that do not delay now friend, leave soon, I will not be able to handle them till now. Kosh Singh, even at that time, Akhilya did not listen to him because he could have left his friend, how could he have left a friend who was his entire family. After all, Arsh knew that if we had even a little Because of delay, the soldiers of Katliya city will attack us, that's why he said those words which he should not have said and as soon as he heard the words of those words in Akhilya's ears, he could not rock even after telling himself at that time? At that time every fear of his fear had gone away from him when he was leaving Arsh, his feet were angry with him at the same time. Th was present, Akhlia said goodbye to her quadrilateral, Arsh gave her share of happiness to her pain, who was probably never going to return, when Sanki crossed his square, then Arsh stopped them all. He had never tried it, when his bail came in front of him, he was broken because Arsh and Akhilya even though Sarerer Seh was different, feet were exactly alike, after all, his soldiers and Raja Ram Pratap took him captive and She was given in such a prison part, whose hurt had been torn every limit of humanity, foot Akhilya did not know this at all and at the time of returning to home ,even Kosh Singh could not return because she too was imprisoned in some kafas. Who was the right foot that is keeping someone safe in one part and in the other giving advice to every day for the pain which he was unable to bear, Raja Ram Pratap sent his army first to find Akhilya Was stationed in the state, at the time, neither did Arsh give any news of Akhilaiya, nor was his pain heard in his pain and on the other side Akhilya Who was also compelled to be so close to Arsh, he could never free him from the dead body He was so brave because he was so brave that he could free himself from his sin, why didn't he do this, why was he forced to bear every tale of pain at the time? A few days later this The news was spread in the whole of Katliya Nagar that Raja Ram Pratap had ordered that Arsh should be burnt in front of the people of Katliya Nagar by cutting each of its parts into pieces, because this was the last donation due to which Perhaps Akhilya could have come in front of the eyes of Raja Ram Lakhan Pratap, feet, it was really the truth in the conversation, this thing was also not known to anyone at the time. It was burning whose storm might have destroyed the city of Katliya. And to find his friend, he made Raj Kumari Kaveri tied, that too with the help of a letter, he says that some roads look straight, so the legs are never straight, the legs are never straight, how did this surgery happen undefined After all, as hey dear, Raja Ram Pratap came to know that he had thought at this time that if princess Kaveri got even a small scratch, he would kill Arsh and in the words of this hatred, Akhilya also thought this. It was taken that if his friend got even a small scratch now, he would kill the princess, now such a beginning has started that those who had killers were also forced and those who did not have killers were also forced because the king of Akhlia Ram Lakhan was the weakness of Partap and Raja Ram Pratap now had both the border legs of Akhilya and perhaps the fire of his vengeance was also stationed a front foot. Had attacked means that the face whose words had been two-sided for some time, now her nature had become the custom of Fana in one part, the feet were asking for a question.It is a matter of fact that if he could have made Princess Kaveri tied to his own palace, then why did he not present her to Arsh at that time, after all, in which part of Arsh is present, which despite being in front, he refuses to free her. has been undefined and now after all who is going to come to the right Fana Katliya Nagar foot and will Akhilya ever be able to get her friend free from the Kafas of King Ram Pratap undefined and Princess Kaveri really loved Akhilya that even behind it There was some enmity involved, and Akhilya knew this, then why did he not come to save Arsh and what were the right things that Arsh told him that he left without saying anything and after all, why did Arsh say this to Akhliya? The princess is waiting for him undefined because she was neither there nor was she waiting for him undefined And if Arsh could free himself from the curse then why is he still bound and every legend of his existence is pinned why It is undefined and the question that is bothering everyone is that is Akhilya able to protect her friend now? undefined Will they be able to earn the release of male prison then , both of them will become famous in the same way as their father in the tradition of male tomb which is recommended by God.

"She says that the beginning of hatred may be one sided
But her need is same in both the parts.

Every identity of my childhood is famous in those memories but one sided
But people nowadays give the name of relationship instead of friendship in both the halves."

there are also many stories which have neither beginning nor end ,still they become so famous in the memories whose words are realated to it . that mystery gets attached to us in such a way that we cannot even try to remove it from ourselves by saying .

9 798887 171654

Printed by Libri Plureos GmbH in Hamburg,
Germany